BOOK #5

OTTO UNDERCOVER

★ THE BRINK OF EX-STINK-TION ★

RHEA PERLMAN

ILLUSTRATED BY

DAN SANTAT

KATHERINE TEGEN BOOKS
An Imprint of HarperCollinsPublishers

Thanks, Mr. Saning'o Uta—
my friend and a true
Maasai warrior

Otto Undercover #5: The Brink of Ex-stink-tion

Text copyright © 2007 by Rhea Perlman

Illustrations copyright © 2007 by Dan Santat

www.harpercollinschildrens.com

Library of Congress Cataloging-in-Publication Data is available.

ISBN-10: 0-06-075503-2 (pbk.) —ISBN-13: 978-0-06-075503-4 (pbk.)

ISBN 10: 0-06-075504-0 (trade bdg.)—ISBN-13: 978-0-06-075504-1 (trade bdg.)

Typography by Jennifer Heuer

1 2 3 4 5 6 7 8 9 10

First Edition

CONTENTS

USEFUL INFORMATION

eye
Eee YiiiY Eee

SECRET FILES

Alias: Otto Pillip
Occupations:
· Secret Agent
· Racecar Driver
· Inventor
· Singer/Songwriter
Problem Area: Can Only Sing the Note G
Legal Guardians: The Aunts
Hobby: Words...Especially Palindromes, Anagrams, and Backward Words

JAKE EBOY

Occupations:
· Senior Secret Agents
Immediate Family:
· Son, Jake Eboy
Whereabouts: On the Lam

ELEANOR AND HOGARTH EBOY

AUNT FOOFOO AKA AUNT OOFOOF

Alias: Uncle FroFro AKA Uncle OrfOrf

Occupations:
- Assistant Secret Agent
- Pit Crew Co-Chief

Hobby: World-Famous Chef

AUNT FIFI AKA AUNT IFIF

Alias: Uncle FriFri AKA Uncle IrfIrf

Occupations:
- Assistant Secret Agent
- Pit Crew Co-Chief

Hobbies: Tap Dancing/Singing

Problem Area: Can Only Sing the Note A-flat

RACECAR

Designer: Otto Pillip
Driver: Otto Pillip
Feature: Fastest Car on Earth

Special Features:
- Claw
- Vacu-Zap
- Voice Command
- A Million More Things

Extra-Special Feature: Can Morph into Other Vehicles

GADGETS

A. Pocket Watch Remote Control **B.** Multi-Functional Radar Tracking and Guiding Ring with Infrared Flashlight **C.** Solar/Lunar Power Helmet **D.** Computer Shoe **E.** Freckle/Pimple 2-Way Global Positioning Transmitters **F.** Kangaroo Jumping Shoes

USELESS INFORMATION

Two Things You Should Know Besides How to Pick Your Nose Without Anyone Seeing and How to Look Like You Coughed up a Hair Ball

1. Palindromes

are words that are spelled exactly the same way backward and forward.

EXAMPLES:

Otto, Racecar, and **butt tub**

2. Anagrams

are words that become other words when their letters are all scrambled up.

EXAMPLES:

the eyes is an anagram for **they see**

the earthquakes is an anagram for **that queer shake**

Beware of the Word *Fart*

This book contains the word *fart* 31 times. If you think the word *fart* is a bad word, or the word *fart* makes you sick and dizzy, tear this page up and do not read past page 38. If you think that *fart* is just another word describing a natural gas that is emitted from the body of almost every animal on the planet, then proceed. With caution.

Get Me Out of Here

There was nothing that drove Otto crazier than having to sit in a theater, wearing "nice clothes," waiting for a play called *HMS Pinafore, or The Lass That Loved a Sailor* to begin, and then having to listen to a bunch of bad songs, including one titled "I'm Called Little Buttercup."

But that's exactly what he was doing.

And it was his birthday.

Donod, L'il, and Mellem are palindromes.

THE PRELUDE

A Birthday Present

The play was his aunt FiFi's idea of a great present. Otto would rather have gone driving with **L'il Mellem**, who was his favorite small baby in the world, or been jamming with **Mellem**'s dad, **Donod**, who played the drums in their band, the Screaming Oranges. Aunt FooFoo couldn't wait to get home and bake 200 different delicious birthday cakes.

But FiFi was so excited about being there. Otto didn't want to make her feel bad. He secretly wished that the electrical power in the theater would go out, and the play would be called off.

Something better happened. Otto opened his program.

It read:

CHAPTER 1

The End

"Are there any animals in this play?" Otto whispered to Aunt FooFoo.

"I don't think so," she said.

"That's what I thought. C'mon, we just got a message. We're going on a mission." Otto stood up.

"We have to leave," whispered FooFoo to her sister. "There are no animals in this play. We're going on a mission."

They got up and started pushing their way through the row.

FiFi's hearing aid wasn't working very well, and she thought FooFoo had said something else. She was outraged.

"There are cannibals in this play, and they're kissing," said FiFi loudly, following them out of the theater.

The rest of the audience heard that and they all got up and began walking out.

The curtain went up. The actors on-stage saw the entire audience leaving and thought that they had time-traveled to the end of the play. They took a bow.

The curtain came down.

CHAPTER 2

Five Minutes to Africa

"Where are we going?" asked FooFoo as they jumped into Racecar and Otto put the pedal to the metal.

"The program said, *A Sad Animal, Act One*, which is an anagram for *Maasailand, at once*. I know that the Maasai are a tribe of people in Africa, but I'm not sure exactly where Maasailand is," said Otto. He punched the letters into Racecar's world Global Positioning System (GPS) system.

FiFi spoke to the police on her cell phone. "I tell you there are kissing cannibals at the theater and they should all be arrested before they start eating each other's lips off."

"There it is," said Otto. "Maasailand

is in the Great Rift Valley of Kenya and
Tanzania, in East Africa."

"There's a plane leaving in five minutes,"
said Otto. "Hold on, we only have until
the next page to get there."

"But . . . ," said The Aunts.

CHAPTER 3

The Next Page

The three secret agents were on a plane to Nairobi, the biggest city in Kenya.

The Aunts were in disguise as The Uncles, and once again, Racecar had been transformed into Racecar Concentrate, a charm in the shape of a racecar. Otto was wearing him around his neck.

The flight was incredibly long. The Aunts were perfectly happy watching the movie, eating, sleeping, and moving their seats backward and forward.

Otto didn't know how he was going to sit in his seat for so many hours. Luckily, right before the plane took off, the oxygen mask compartments opened up and all the masks came down. There was a lot of pandemonium, but nothing was really wrong. No one noticed that attached to Otto's mask was a computer disc. No doubt the whole event was rigged by the agency Otto worked for . . . Eee YiiiY Eee.

He inserted the disc into his shoe computer. That's how he learned the facts about

SMELLDON O'DOR
Alias: Smelldon P. Yoo
The Facts:
- Smelldon looks like a skunk.
- Smelldon lives in a port-o-potty.
- Smelldon thinks he's gorgeous.
- Smelldon smells.

There was also another photo on the disc, of a smiling Maasai man. The man held the knuckle of his index finger under his *eye*. Otto had a strong feeling that the man was an Eee YiiiY Eee secret agent, and that perhaps the finger under the *eye* was some kind of secret sign.

Eye is a palindrome.

18

CHAPTER 4

Who Cut the . . . ?

"We're just over Tanzania, making our descent into Nairobi," said the pilot. "On your left you can see the snowy top of Mount Kilimanjaro, and the plains of the Serengeti. . . . PEEUUW!!!!!"

Just then a huge stink wafted through the aircraft, which veered sharply to the right.

"Sorry, folks, we're going to try another approach. Hold your noses, please," mumbled the pilot.

Otto looked out the window. He could see the massive plains where the animals should be roaming freely, only there was no movement down there. The whole area was covered by a steamy gas.

CHAPTER 5

Secret Sign

The Nairobi airport buzzed with a swarm of people. Some waved signs with names on them. They were there to greet the passengers getting off the plane.

One of these greeters was a tall black man. Leaning on a spear, he stood on one leg, like a stork. A bright red fabric draped his body, and beautiful beaded jewelry snaked around his arms and neck. He looked strong and serious, especially compared

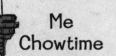

Me chowtime is an anagram for Come with me.

with his sign, which said, "*Me Chowtime*."

"Oh, that man must be here for us," said Aunt FooFoo. "I'm starving."

Otto recognized him instantly. He was the Maasai man on the disc. Otto glanced at him and held the knuckle of his index finger up to his *eye*. The man smiled and did the same. Then he turned over the sign. It said, "*Come with me*."

Otto's hunch was right. The man was another operative working for Eee YiiiY Eee.

CHAPTER 6

An Ox That Isn't a Moron

"My name is *Ayamaya*," said the man.

"I'm Otto," said Otto.

"*Supai ero*," said *Ayamaya*. "That means 'hello, boy' in my language, which is called Maa. We also speak Swahili. '*Jambo*' is 'hello' in Swahili." He walked in great strides out of the airport. "We must hurry."

"Thanks for the lesson," said Otto. "These are my uncles, FroFro and FriFri, but I call them *OrfOrf* and *IrfIrf*. Hurrying is our specialty. Did you know that your name and my name are both spelled the same way backward and forward?" he added.

"Yes, that is called a palindrome," said *Ayamaya*.

"You speak very good English," said

Otto. "Hardly anyone knows that word, even if they've gone to school for 20 years and are doctors."

"*Wow*," said *Ayamaya*.

"*Huh*?" said FiFi.

"*Hah*," said FooFoo.

Ayamaya nodded toward The Uncles and said, "How about oxymoron?"

"I don't care how smart you are, you have no right to call my brother an ox and me a moron," said FiFi.

"He's not, Uncle *IrfIrf*. An oxymoron is what you call two words that go together but are opposites. Like *long shorts*."

"Yes, or *pretty ugly*," said *Ayamaya* delightedly.

"Now you're asking for it," said FiFi. "I told you to lay off the insults."

"Come with me," said FooFoo, taking *Ayamaya*'s arm. "I'm the pretty one . . . when I'm not a handsome man, I mean."

24

Otto dropped the Racecar Concentrate charm into a mixture of fizzy water and yeast. An instant later, *Mission Racecar* was standing in front of them.

They got in and powered out of the airport.

CHAPTER 7

Eat and Run

"We have a very big and disgusting problem," explained *Ayamaya*. "The land of my people and of many, many animals has been taken over by a terrible skunk-man. We must go there quickly."

Otto set Racecar's GPS to Maasailand, and switched into *Hyper-Speed*.

"This is a very fast car, like the cheetah," said *Ayamaya*, "and it smells *awfully good*, not like other cars or the skunk-man."

"That's because it's powered by a special mixture of espresso coffee, Tabasco sauce, and chili pepper oil, instead of gasoline," said Otto.

"That sounds very delicious," said *Ayamaya*. "Maybe if I drank it, I, too, could run as fast as the cheetah." He laughed.

"Yes," said FooFoo. "I have a small glass of it every morning and I do everything fast. I also have some nice eggs and sardines over easy, and some nice butterscotch baked clams and onions, and a slice of liver bread, nice. Ottie, please pull over at the next coffee shop. I'm starving."

Otto might have done just that except they had left Nairobi and were now in Tanzania on the outskirts of Maasailand, and there wasn't a coffee shop to be found.

CHAPTER 8

The End of the Road

Thousands of Maasai people crowded the streets and the road. Many looked sick. None looked happy.

"This is not yet Maasailand," said *Ayamaya*. "It is the city of Arusha. We cannot go any farther."

"Why not?" asked Otto.

"If we do, we may die," said *Ayamaya*. "The spray of the skunk-man is destroying everything in the bush. We got out, but all our cows and the wild animals are still there."

"Are they all dead?" asked Otto, alarmed.

"No, the skunk-man lets off just enough of the stink juice to keep them unconscious," said *Ayamaya*. "I will tell you the worst part in a flashback. Are you ready?"

"Wait a minute," said FooFoo. "I have an itch on my foot." She took off her shoe and scratched.

CHAPTER 9

Sort of Ready

"That's better," she said.

"Good," said *Ayamaya*.

"Wait a minute. Now I have one on the other foot."

11 Itches Later

FooFoo was ready.

"I'm ready," she said.

But FiFi had fallen asleep and was snoring loudly.

"FriFri, wake up," shouted FooFoo.

"I'm all ears," said FiFi, startled.

"That's not exactly true," said FooFoo, "because you are eyes and a body and a head and lips too, and even one of your ears is out of order."

"You're chubby," said FiFi.

His aunts seemed to be done talking.

"Okay, we're really ready now," said Otto.

AYAMAYA'S FLASHBACK

"Five days ago a large port-o-potty drove across Maasailand. Out of its window sailed slices of pizza. Soon thousands, maybe millions of hungry lions, leopards, giraffes, elephants, wildebeests, and creatures of all kinds followed close behind.

"My people have many cows. We trade them, drink their milk, and eat their meat. Cows are everything to us. But they all ran off with the other pizza-loving animals.

"I had to see what was happening. I crept silently alongside the animals,

keeping myself well hidden.

"When the port-o-potty stopped, the animals howled like crazy for more pizza. Then I heard a toilet flushing inside and a voice yelling, 'Keep your pants on, I'm coming.' The door opened, and out leaped a small man, **barely dressed**, wearing only a pair of tight **long shorts**. Everywhere else on his body was black and white hair, like a skunk. Even on his face.

"'Pipe down, youse good-for-nothin' lumps,' he bellowed.

"He pumped a squeezer, which was attached to a tube coming from under his hairy chest. His body rumbled and erupted into what sounded like the volcanic release of intestinal gas. Then, a gray mist sprayed forcefully into the air.

"A huge stink was carried by the wind and entered the nostrils of every living thing for miles around, including my own.

"The animals, being so close to the toxic fumes, stumbled and collapsed on the ground, breathing, but unconscious.

"The Maasai people coughed and gagged and ran as fast as they could away from the smell. I barely had the strength to move, but I forced my legs to carry me.

"As I ran, I could hear the skunk-man saying, '"Step right up, step right up, welcome to the one, the only, Skunkland Zoo

of the World. Youse mutts is the first inhab-
itants. I am Smelldon O'Dor, and I am the
big stinky cheese around here. Youse can
all bow down to me. Oh, that's right, youse
already are. Ha ha ha, just a little zoo joke.'

"He tipped his hat.

"'Pleased to eat ya. Ha ha ha, just
kidding. Pleased to meet ya. Step right

up and have a free sample of my Genuine Authentic Secret Elixir of youth, strength, and especially beauty. Also guaranteed to remove unwanted pimples and make you do the splits. Step right up."

"No one stepped up, so Smelldon let out another loud *toot*.

"The animals just lay there.

"'Youse guys is out like a light.'

"He walked among the unconscious creatures, stopping every once in a while to tap his squeezer.

"'From now on youse mutts don't gotta hunt or do any of that there roamin' in the bush. Youse can just relax and put your tootsies up, while my wife builds youse cages and feeds youse a balanced diet of fortified stink juice.

"'Soon your ugly fur will fall off, and youse will sprout beautiful black and white hair, just like my own, and all of youse species will become extinct. Instead, youse will become mighty skunks unlike the world has ever seen before. People will come from far and wide to see the magnificent Sku-lions, Sku-leopards, and Sku-rhinos. Then they'll sniff my fart spray and they will become Sku-humans. I'll have their cages ready.

"'Smelldon's Stench will spread all over the globe when I open Skunkland 2, 3, and 400 million thousand. The whole joint will be a zoo and I'll be the zookeeper boss of the world, and no one will have to breathe flowers or baby powder or freshly baked bread no more.'

"Smelldon farted for six whole minutes.

"'Ahh, delicious! Stink a dink a dink a dink a dink a stink a doo,' he sang. 'I love mee.'"

FooFoo fainted for a second. She woke up, shaking.

"The freshly baked bread thing was too much for my sister," said FiFi. "You gave her a *chilling fever*."

"Who is Smelldon's wife?" asked Otto.

"He doesn't have one yet. He has tried a lot of dating services but is still waiting for the woman of his dreams."

Chilling fever is an oxymoron.

41

"Is this the skunk-man?" asked Otto. He showed them a printout of the picture of Smelldon.

Everyone gasped.

"Yes, that is the **butt-head**," said **Ayamaya**.

"We have to pay him a visit without getting ourselves killed," said Otto. "Help me, **IrfIrf**."

FiFi plugged in a lightbulb and held it over Otto's head.

He immediately got an idea.

He looked around him, then whispered to *Ayamaya* and The Aunts, "It's not likely, but there may be *seips* in this crowd. Get in the car. I'll give you the *nalp* in *edoc*."

Seips is backward for spies. Nalp is backward for plan. Edoc is backward for code.

CHAPTER 11

The Nalp in Edoc

Otto whispered, "We'll turn the *arc* into a *petal ben*."

Arc is an anagram for car. Petal ben is an anagram for elephant.

CHAPTER 12

The Elecar

"This is not a **doog nalp**," said **Ayamaya**, upset. "Aside from the sneaky buffalo, the **petal hen** is our **least favorite** animal. Why not turn it into a **fear fig**, who is a much better neighbor to the Maasai people. The **petal hen**s like to trample all our grass and drink all our water. The good **fear fig**s use only what they need."

"Don't worry," said Otto. "This **petal hen** is very friendly and won't hurt anything."

Otto pressed his shoelace to *Option 22.* Racecar's frame melted and morphed into the shape of a baby-size elephant.

The inside of the car was outfitted like a surveillance truck, with TV monitors, sensitive sound equipment, and a laboratory.

"I call this the Elecar. Nothing can penetrate it. We will be protected from the smell as long as we stay inside," said Otto.

Ayamaya was delighted. "Did you know that the word for 'elephant' in Maa is *alalala*?"

The sound of that word reminded FiFi of a song. She started doing her vocal exercises, singing the note of A-flat over and over.

"The Elecar is adorable," said Aunt FooFoo. "Can I give him some peanuts?"

"Yes," said Otto, "if you have any."

FooFoo pulled a bag of nuts out of her sleeve and held it up to the Elecar's trunk, which was on his *front end*. The nuts were sucked in, ground up, and poured out of a chute as peanut butter.

FooFoo made peanut-butter patties with ketchup and onions, which she pulled out of her other sleeve.

"We'd better eat," said Otto. "We're going to need our strength for the mission."

CHAPTER 13

Lions and Zebras and Cows, Oh My

Otto put the Elecar into *Hyper-Speed*. Seconds later they were in Maasailand.

It was a dreary sight. The plains were dry and brown, a sickly haze hanging over everything.

The animals were still sprawled all over the ground. Something had changed, though. New black and white hair spotted their normal fur.

In the middle of everything stood the gigantic port-o-potty. Lettering on the side said "Smelldon's Stinkwagon."

Smelldon sat outside on a lounge chair

49

next to his garden of beans and cabbage, which was all he ate. Holding up a mirror, he gazed longingly at his reflection, while brushing his face, making his hair shiny. He was a real *ladies' man*.

CHAPTER 14

The Ideas Keep Coming

"Now what?" asked everyone.

"Lightbulb, please," said Otto.

FiFi held one over Otto's head.

"I've got it!" he cried instantly.

CHAPTER 15

The Nalp-Part Two

Otto took out his remote and gave Racecar a *voice command.*

"Play dead," he whispered.

The Elecar folded up its leg wheels and lay down.

"My research tells me that Smelldon is very vain," explained Otto, "so I will act like an important scientist from Germany who is here to give him an award.

"*Ayamaya* will pretend to be our guide, but his real job will be to relay information back to *IrfIrf* in the Elecar. I think it would be good to have a woman with us, so *OrfOrf*, you can change into a dress."

"That plan is *awfully good*!" said *Ayamaya*.

"*IrfIrf*, you man the car," said Otto. "Actually, you can woman the car because I need your beard and mustache."

"But if we take off our disguises, *Ayamaya* will know that I am a woman named FooFoo who you call *OofOof* instead of a man named FroFro who you call *OrfOrf*," FooFoo whispered to Otto.

"He may also find out that my brother FriFri who you call *IrfIrf* is really my sister FiFi who you call *IfIf*."

Otto hadn't told his aunts that *Ayamaya* worked for Eee Yiiiy Eee, and that he already knew they were secret agents in disguise. It was more fun to tease them.

"That's a chance we'll have to take," he whispered back.

CHAPTER 16

The Team

"Smelldon O'Dor," called Otto. He spoke in a pretty bad German accent.

"It is Dr. Otto Von Schnitzelfarfer here. I have come to see you with my team from the No Bells or Whistles Peace Prize Committee."

Leaping up from his

armchair, Smelldon boomed, "Where in the sam hill are ya?" His hand slid menacingly to his fart pump.

"We are here beside this ***mostly dead*** elephant. You must promise not to spritz us with the stink or we can't come with the prize," said Otto.

"Okay, 86 on the spritz," said Smelldon.

"Promise, and swear, and cross your

heart and hope to die?" asked Otto.

"Stick a needle in my *eye*," said Smelldon excitedly. He really wanted the prize.

"We're going in," said Otto to the team. "Remember to flatter him as much as possible."

"We are coming," called Otto.

"**Won't I be bit now**?" whispered FooFoo, afraid of the animals.

"I will protect you," said *Ayamaya*.

FooFoo batted her eyelashes and took his arm.

The three of them stepped out of the Elecar.

Won't I be bit now is a palindrome.

The Stinkmaker

"It is an honor to meet such a wonderful scientist," said Otto, shaking Smelldon's hairy hand. "This is my colleague, Dr. Von Strudelmeister," he said, introducing his aunt.

"What beautiful hair you have all over your body and face. I've tried to grow mine, but it always stops when it gets to my forehead," said FooFoo.

"And this is our guide, Mr. Saning'o Uta," continued Otto.

"On behalf of my people, we are so happy you parked your beautiful bathroom in our neighborhood. All the children now want one of their own," said *Ayamaya*.

"You said it, bud. I love the little tots. Bring 'em by anytime for a jolt of juice.

Where's the prize?" asked Smelldon.

"Well, to tell you the truth, I made a little fib before," said Otto.

"What d'ya mean?" asked Smelldon, his eyes darkening and his hair standing on end.

"Actually, you have been nominated for the prize for Most Outstanding Stench, but so has one other stinkmaker in Jamaica. We have to prove that your stink is the most stinkiest," said Otto.

"Take my word for it, it's the stinkiest," said Smelldon.

Just then a buffalo stirred and stood up.

Smelldon pointed his finger at the buffalo, and pumped the squeezer. There was a loud fart sound, and a puff of gas sprayed out of his finger and surrounded the animal, who tottered on his feet and collapsed onto the ground.

"Isn't that wonderful," said Otto. "You farted from your finger."

Then a leopard tried to stand. Smelldon pointed his knee at it, pressed the squeezer, and the same thing happened.

"It is remarkable. I will tell the committee that you are a genius gas-meister."

"You ain't seen nothin' yet," bragged Smelldon. "I can fart from every pore on my skin." Then he put his finger to his nose and gave himself a little wiff.

"Want some?" he asked generously.

"No, no, thank you anyway," said Otto, backing up. "We will just ask you

a few simple questions, and that will be that. May we come into your outhouse?"

"Yeah, yeah," said Smelldon, "but make it snappy. I'm very busy. I got the whole world to destroy."

"What?" asked Otto.

"I said, I got the whole world to enjoy," he lied.

"I will stay out here, and keep an *eye* on the animals," said *Ayamaya*, happy to have an excuse not to enter the Stinkwagon.

CHAPTER 18

Fit for a King

"**Wow**," said Otto, holding his nose. "This is some port-o-potty."

"It's a **little big**, like a port-o-palace," said FooFoo, gagging. "But very homey at the same time." It was huge, with mirrors everywhere. Piles of garbage covered the floor. The actual toilet was a throne.

Smelldon sat down on a compost heap and applied hair gel to his chest.

"Let's get down to business," said Otto. "Tell us a little bit about your work."

"Why should I?" asked Smelldon suspiciously.

"Do you want the prize?" asked Otto.

"What is it anyway?" asked Smelldon.

"A zillion dollars, a round-trip ticket for two to Miami Beach, Florida, a brand-new washer and dryer, and Mirror, Mirror on the Wall from *Snow White*."

"Jackpot!!!" said Smelldon, throwing handfuls of garbage in the air. "I want it. I want it."

CHAPTER 19

Gross

"This here is my laboratory," said Smelldon. He led them to an indoor pit of bubbling filth-muck.

"And this here stink juice is my elixir of life." He dipped in a cup, drank the liquid, and belched loudly. The smell from the burp nearly knocked Otto and FooFoo off their feet.

"**Wow**, that is a spectacular mixture," said Otto.

"And powerful, too, so don't mess with it. A little bit can turn youse into a gorgeous creature like myself, but a little extra, and you'll be pushin' up daisies. Not that there'll be any daisies left to push up."

"Oh, I love daisies," said Aunt FooFoo.

"He means we'll be dead," said Otto.

"Oh, I hate dead," said Aunt FooFoo.

"Say, do either of youse professor types know a way to cook beans and cabbage besides boiling it?" asked Smelldon.

"Well, yes, I have written a book on the subject," said FooFoo. "It's called *3008 Ways to Cook Beans and Cabbage*. Let me tell you some of the recipes."

"Sure, doll. Let's check out our mugs in the mirror and brush our fur while we shoot the breeze," said Smelldon.

While they chatted, Otto snuck a vial out of his pocket and carefully filled it with a sample of Smelldon's stink juice.

CHAPTER 20

Stink Juice Relay

Smelldon and FooFoo were in deep conversation, so Otto was free to open the door to the Stinkwagon without being seen. He handed the vial to *Ayamaya*.

"Send this down the Eletrunk. FiFi will analyze it," said Otto. "We need to know what's in the juice and how it's activated."

"Right away," said *Ayamaya*. "I'm sure we will have our answer in the *near future*."

Near future is an oxymoron.

CHAPTER 21

Recipe for Disaster

FiFi poured the juice into Otto's Certified Centrifugal Scent Separator. It didn't take long to see what it was made of.

FiFi spoke to Otto through her headset. "Rotten eggs, stale cigarettes, manure, garbage, Limburger cheese, bus fumes, dead fish, barf, and pure skunk ooze."

Those are all very smelly things, thought Otto. Pure skunk ooze on its own can practically kill a person. Smelldon can fart from every

pore on his skin, so the stink juice must be hooked into his sweat glands, and there are 2.6 million sweat glands in the body. *But how is he able to fart so powerfully?* he wondered.

"How much cabbage do you eat at once?" FooFoo asked Smelldon.

"24 heads," he answered, "and a bushel of beans."

That's it, thought Otto. The sulfur gas from the beans and cabbage, mixed with the other ingredients, creates magnaforce farts. With that vat of stink juice, he has enough gas to cover the entire planet.

"My recipe calls for a wheelbarrow full of cabbage, a bucket of my world-famous barbecue sauce, served over a hill of mashed beans. One taste and you'll be so happy you'll want to marry me," said FooFoo.

"I do," said Smelldon.

"You do what?" asked FooFoo.

"I do want to marry you," said Smelldon.

"I do too," said FooFoo, jumping into his fluffy arms.

CHAPTER 22

There Goes the Bride

"Dr. Von Strudelmeister and I must be going now," said Otto, grabbing FooFoo's arm.

"Aren't you happy for me, Ottie, I mean Dr. Von Schnitzelfever?" asked FooFoo. "The theme of the wedding will be springtime under the African skies, and we'll have bunches and bunches of beautiful flowers."

"Dead ones," interrupted Smelldon.

"Yes, darling," said FooFoo. "And everyone will throw rice."

"Beans," said Smelldon. "Hey Schnitzelfarfer, why don't ya stick around for the wedding?" asked Smelldon. "Youse can be the dead flower boy."

That's what I'm afraid of, thought Otto.

"We have come to the conclusion that no one can have a stinkier smell than you," he said out loud. "The deadline for the contest is 3:00 this afternoon. Dr. Von Strudelmeister and I must give our results to the committee immediately or you will forfeit the prize. Good-bye and thank you very much for letting us stand in your garbage."

"Relax. This here ceremony is only gonna take a couple of minutes. What's-her-name over here has to get to work buildin' cages and cookin' my cabbage," said

Smelldon. "How's about I give youse a makeover so youse look more spiffy for the wedding. I'll start with your facial hair."

Smelldon lunged and ran his brush through Otto's fake beard. It pulled right off his face.

"Hey, you and the dame ain't on the level," said Smelldon, enraged. "Youse is liars. Put an egg in ya' shoes and beat it."

He grabbed his fart-squeezer. But FooFoo leaped onto Smelldon and tackled him to the ground.

"The engagement is off, you lousy, no good hair ball. I'm leaving you," said FooFoo.

Before Smelldon could get his footing, Otto and FooFoo ran out of the Stinkwagon.

CHAPTER 23

A Near Miss

Otto, FooFoo, and *Ayamaya* jumped into the Elecar and took off.

CHAPTER 24

The Chase Begins

The Stinkwagon took off after them.

CHAPTER 25

Let Her Rip

"He's chasing us," said *Ayamaya*.

"Good," said Otto. "We'll lead him on a wild ride. It'll give us some time to develop a stink eradicator."

"I will set a course that will drive the skunk-man crazy," said *Ayamaya*. "Of course, you will have to drive like crazy too."

"*Ayamaya*, secret agenting is my job, but racecar driving is my passion. Let me have it."

"You chumps'll never get away in that pitiful pachyderm," yelled Smelldon out his window. "Have a dose of this." He farted through his hand at the Elecar. The juice hit, and ran down the side.

Otto switched gears and cranked the

speed up to 90 mph, which was slow for Racecar, but he didn't want Smelldon to fall too far behind.

The Stinkwagon kept up the pace behind Otto.

"Ottie, I have an *awfully good* idea about how to get rid of the smell," said FooFoo. "Flower power."

"You mean from the hippies in the 1960s?" asked Otto.

"Yes. Everybody wore flowers in their hair and danced around while singing songs about peace and love. I was a hippie then too. It was impossible to resist the power of the flower."

"I did," said FiFi.

"That's true, but you were having a bad sinus infection for about six years and couldn't smell anything," said FooFoo.

"Yes, I missed the whole summer of love, and the winter, and all the other seasons. That's why I'm a bitter, cranky little woman today," said FiFi sadly.

"I think you're **terribly nice**, and only a little **sweet and sour**," said *Ayamaya*, patting her on the head.

"Thank you," said FiFi shyly. Her eyes lit up like two glowing lightbulbs.

That gave Otto an idea.

CHAPTER 26

Otto's Idea

"*FART FORCE FIELD,*"

said Otto.

82

CHAPTER 27

Ayamaya's Question

"What's a fart force field?" asked *Ayamaya*.

"It's a big bubble made of super-strength air freshener that goes around you and protects you from fatal fart fumes," said Otto.

"Do we have one?" asked *Ayamaya*.

CHAPTER 28

Otto's Answer

"NO!"

replied Otto.

CHAPTER 29

Over the Potholes and Through the Mud

"That is a rough break," said *Ayamaya*.

"Hit me with another lightbulb," said Otto.

FiFi took out the bulb just as Elecar went over a huge bump in the road. She dropped it, and it broke.

"Whoops," she said.

"Major whoops," said FooFoo. "That was our last one."

"Nobody panic," said Otto. "We just have to keep driving around while I do some quick thinking."

Just then the Stinkwagon pulled alongside Racecar.

"Whatsa matter, Dumbo, did ya forget how to fly?" sneered Smelldon.

Otto put his foot on the accelerator and peeled out at 150 mph.

CHAPTER 30

Driving in Circles

The terrain of Maasailand was extremely rough. There were few roads. Many had been washed out by floods during the rainy season. There were huge ruts and rocks everywhere. *Ayamaya* had set a challenging circular course. On a scale of 1 to 10, it was a 65.

"Hey *Ayamaya*, have you Maasais ever thought of opening a racetrack around here? It would be *serious fun*!" said Otto.

Ayamaya laughed loudly. "We Maasais don't have cars. We walk everywhere, even if it is 50 miles away. Aside from the skunk-man, automobile smell is our *least favorite*. Except for the perfume found on many women and inside magazines."

Just then Racecar hit a mountain of

Serious fun is an oxymoron.

mud and came banging down on the other side of it, landing in a narrow rocky river.

Amazingly, the Stinkwagon was right behind them.

"Hey buds, I'm gonna make youse famous. Youse is gonna be the first Sku-humans in my zoo. It's an opportunity of a lifetime," yelled Smelldon, letting out another major fart. A nearby termite mound immediately flattened to the ground.

CHAPTER 31

Slow Quick Thinking

The chase continued for laps and laps, and miles and miles. Day turned to night. Night turned to day. Day turned to night again. Every once in a while, Smelldon would stop to refuel the Stinkwagon. He was carrying plenty of gasoline with him. When that happened, Otto stopped too. The Aunts would do a quick pit check of Elecar. Then FooFoo would whip up another peanut delight, and FiFi kept everyone's spirits up by singing "The elephant's trunk swings steady and slow" in the note of A-flat.

"**Good grief**," said FooFoo, glaring at her sister. "That song is giving me a **terrific headache**. Ottie, have you thought of a stink eradicator yet?"

"Almost," said Otto. His brain was practically exploding from thinking so hard.

"We are very near the volcano called Ol Doinyo Lengai," said *Ayamaya*. "It is a sacred place to the Maasais."

"That's where we should put him," said FooFoo. "If he farts there, he'll explode. I

know that because I once served a cauli-flower soufflé to Coco, the famous leaping circus clown, and he farted just as he was jumping through the hoop of fire. He went up in flames, but luckily, Jojo, the famous seltzer bottle circus clown, was nearby and he put out the fire, saving Coco's life and receiving the Momo the Clown Medal of Honor."

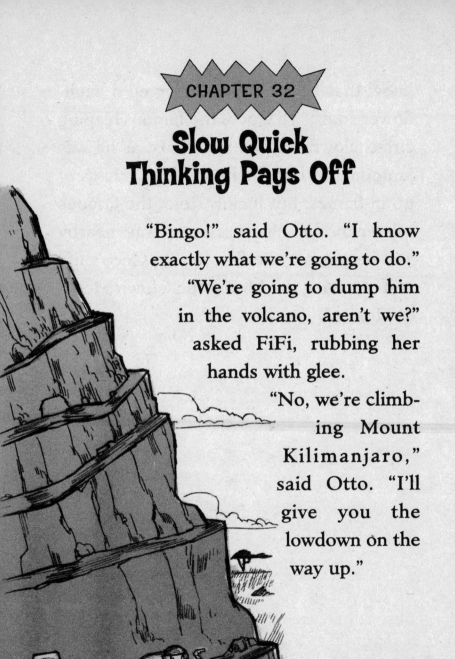

CHAPTER 32

Slow Quick Thinking Pays Off

"Bingo!" said Otto. "I know exactly what we're going to do."

"We're going to dump him in the volcano, aren't we?" asked FiFi, rubbing her hands with glee.

"No, we're climbing Mount Kilimanjaro," said Otto. "I'll give you the lowdown on the way up."

CHAPTER 33

The Lowdown on the Way Up

"When Smelldon swallows the stink juice, it flows into his sweat glands, which are under the pores of his skin. That's why, when he presses the squeezer, the farts can squirt from any part of his body," explained Otto.

He was driving the Elecar in a circular path up Mount Kilimanjaro. Smelldon was close behind.

"Aunt *IfIf*, get out a gallon of our Secret Formula Rubber Cement," said Otto.

"Got it," said FiFi.

"When we get to the top, we'll lure Smelldon out of the Stinkwagon, and before he can let out a fart, I'll spray him with the glue through Racecar's elephant trunk. The cement will work as a Pore Paster, and the farts won't be able to escape through his skin," said Otto.

"I think 'Pore Plaster' sounds better," said FooFoo.

"Or 'Fart Fastener,'" said *Ayamaya*.

"I think we should throw him in the volcano and watch him burn up," said FiFi.

Otto never took the violent option if there was another way to do something, which there always was.

"The cold air outside will instantly freeze the cement. All we need is for someone to get out of Racecar at the top of the mountain, in order to lure Smelldon out of his Stinkwagon. That person will be risking his or her life. Are there any volunteers?" asked Otto.

Silence

There weren't too many volunteers yet.

CHAPTER 35

A Brave Dude

"I am a Maasai warrior," said *Ayamaya*, breaking the silence. "I am not even afraid of lions, much less the gas of a man. I will do it."

"Gee, and I was just about to volunteer," said FiFi.

"Me too," said FooFoo.

"Thanks, *Ayamaya*," said Otto.

He looked back. The Stinkwagon was teetering on the steep slope of Mount Kilimanjaro.

"Uh-oh," said Otto. "That port-o-potty is going to fall back down the mountain."

Keeping his hand on the wheel, Otto gave Racecar a *voice command.*

"Uncoil Tail," he said.

The Elecar's tail stretched out and hooked itself around the grille of the Stinkwagon. Now Racecar was climbing the steep mountain and towing the wagon too. It was a heavy load. Racecar's wheels were losing traction.

"Manual Feet," yelled Otto. Racecar's wheels pulled in, and the strong Elecar legs bent, and then trudged up the mountain step by step.

"I can see the summit," said Otto.

"FiFi, load the trunk."

She poured in the liquid rubber cement. Racecar stopped. The Stinkwagon stopped too.

"*Ayamaya*, are you ready?" asked Otto.

"I'm ready," he said.

Otto took control of the *Trunk Guider and Sprayer*.

"When I yell 'Now,' you make as much noise as possible," he said to The Aunts.

"*Ayamaya* . . . go!" cried Otto.

CHAPTER 36

Fresh Frozen

Ayamaya opened the door of the Elecar and jumped out.

"What, do ya got a screw loose?" said Smelldon. "I'm gonna clobber you with my stench."

"I am not afraid of you," said *Ayamaya*.

"You ain't playin' with a full deck. Don't say I didn't warn ya," shouted Smelldon.

The door to the Stinkwagon opened.

Ayamaya stood up straight.

Smelldon stepped out into the open air.

"Now!" shouted Otto.

FooFoo banged two massive pots together. FiFi screamed in the note of A-flat.

Smelldon turned for a split second toward the sound.

Otto aimed the *Trunk Sprayer* and pumped it full force. A thick stream of rubber cement shot out, covering Smelldon from head to foot, closing all the pores in his hairy skin, then instantly freezing. Only his nostrils and opened mouth were left uncovered.

"Of all the out-houses in all the towns in all the world, youse louses had to walk into mine," croaked Smelldon. Then his tongue froze, so he couldn't talk. That was a relief.

CHAPTER 37

Melted Ice

Otto radioed the Nairobi police. They came in a helicopter, picked up Smelldon, and deposited him on a prison raft in a remote region of the Indian Ocean. There, when the rubber cement melted, he could fart all he wanted and not hurt anything until he ran out of gas, which he would since he had no more juice.

Otto and the team took the vat of stink juice and brought it carefully back down the mountain and over to the crater of the Ol Doinyo Lengai volcano.

For his bravery, they gave *Ayamaya* the honor of pouring it in.

It caused a brilliant fire that lit up the valley for miles.

That's when they saw

CHAPTER 38

Watch Out

the
stampede.

CHAPTER 39

Big Baby

The effects of the stink juice had worn off, and the wild animals were running full force across Maasailand with the elephants in the lead.

"This is a *fine mess*," said *Ayamaya*. "They are out of control. Everyone will be killed."

"No we won't," said Otto.

"Oh goodie," said FooFoo.

Otto ejected his shoe computer. It was still set to *Option 22—Elecar*. He pressed his shoelace to ½ on the menu bar.

"Everyone squish together," he said.

The sides and roof of the Elecar started closing in on them.

"I'm making the Elecar small, because I read in an animal book that adult elephants

won't attack a baby elephant," said Otto.
"Or was that mooses?" he mumbled.

"Who cares?" said FiFi. "We're proba-
bly going to be crushed by this car before
the animals even reach us."

"Couldn't you have made him *medium large*?" gasped FooFoo. The four passengers were pressed so tightly together, they could hardly breathe.

"It's a good thing we're a *small crowd*," gasped *Ayamaya*.

This has to work, thought Otto, crossing his fingers. He would have crossed his toes too, but someone was stepping on them.

CHAPTER 40

Charge!

The team came roaring down the volcano in the Elecar. They rode at *Hyper-Speed* straight toward the stampede.

When they got about 50 yards away, Otto said, "Now I will **start stopping**." He put on the brakes. The little Elecar stopped and just stood there swinging its trunk.

It worked. The elephants in the front line came to a screeching halt. All the animals behind them were forced to

Start stopping is an oxymoron.

stop too, causing a huge pileup of elephants, zebras, giraffes, antelope, hyenas, wildebeests, cheetahs, buffalo, and the rest. Dazed and hungry, they were still a little stinky from all the stink juice Smelldon had sprayed on them, but **much less** than before.

CHAPTER 41

Sock It to Me

"Poor guys, they've been through a lot today. We will herd them back to their grazing places," said *Ayamaya*, eyeing some other Maasai warriors who were now returning to Maasailand. The Maasais were brilliant cattle herders, but this time it was wild animals they were facing. *Ayamaya* was just a teeny bit nervous.

"Wait a minute," said FooFoo.

She got out a spray bottle, filled it with onion, jalapeno pepper, cayenne pepper, castor oil, dish soap, and water. "This will keep the animals from attacking you. They don't like this smell."

"Really?" asked *Ayamaya* and Otto.

"Certainly," said FooFoo.

Ayamaya opened Elecar's door.

"Wait a minute," said FooFoo again. She made a mixture of hydrogen peroxide, baking soda, tomato juice, and dish soap; put it into Elecar's trunk; and sprayed it all over the herd of wild animals.

"That will take the rest of the skunk smell off them," she said.

"It will?" asked Otto and *Ayamaya*.

"Certainly," said FooFoo.

"Why didn't you tell us about that earlier when we could have tried it on the skunk-man?" asked Otto.

"I didn't think we had any tomato juice, but it was just *found missing* in my sock," said FooFoo happily.

"I'll meet you at my home tonight," said *Ayamaya*. "We will celebrate with my family."

"Where do you live?" asked Otto.

"Oh, anywhere," said *Ayamaya*. "We're nomadic, which means we move around a lot. This spot is very roomy and has plenty of grass and water for our cattle. We will live here."

CHAPTER 42

Let Them Eat Cow?

It was the first time since the Un-Prelude of this book that Otto remembered it was his birthday. He was hoping for a big party with lots of music and a huge cake.

He was extremely disappointed to learn that the Maasais don't record the day they were born, so they never celebrate birthdays and never eat cake. In fact, the only things they do eat are milk, honey, cow, goat and sheep meat, and a little corn. They don't eat or grow anything else.

"The cows eat the grass, and we eat the cows. There is no reason to eat vegetables or grains," explained *Ayamaya*.

When Aunt FooFoo heard this, she almost fainted again.

"I know lots of meat recipes," she said,

"but I can't make a cake out of a cow."

Otto felt like fainting himself. He was starving, and sick of peanut butter. He really really wanted a birthday cake.

"Don't you have anything else up your sleeve or in your socks?" he asked hopefully.

"I suppose I could make a cake out of corn and honey," said FooFoo.

"I guess," said Otto sadly.

Just then they all noticed a cloud of dust out in the bush. It was getting bigger and coming toward them.

"I don't think you're gonna be doing much celebrating anyway," said FiFi. "We got rid of the skunk-man, but that there is the dirt-man and he's on his way here! Everybody RUUUUNNN!"

Nobody did, especially not FiFi, who is against exercise and never runs anywhere.

"Duuuuude!" someone called.

Otto couldn't believe his ears, or his eyes. The cloud of dirt turned out to be his friends *Donod* and *L'il Mellem* coming toward them in a jeep.

"Surprise, small racecar dude! Happy birthday to ya!" yelled *Donod*.

"Happy bird day, *L'il* Daddy monkey poo," said *L'il Mellem*, jumping into Otto's arms. He always called Otto *L'il* Daddy, even though he wasn't one.

Otto was waaaaaay happy to see them.

"How did you guys know I was here?" he asked.

"Dude," said *Donod*, pointing to his head, "party *radar*."

"Way," said Otto, amazed.

"Way, way," said *Donod*. "And besides, this old chap English dude put us in a plane and flew us here."

"Mr. *Rabbar*?" asked Otto, getting a warm feeling in the pit of his stomach.

"Yeah, that was it. A gnarly big-butted dude," said *Donod*.

Otto hadn't heard from Mr. *Rabbar* since they had defeated Prune Man together a few missions ago, but he always hoped the old chap would somehow be a part of his life.

"Close your eyes for a big surprise," said *Donod*. "Make sure he doesn't peek, Melvin dude."

CHAPTER 43

Eyes Wide Closed

Otto closed his eyes. He knew exactly what had happened. His parents wanted to make sure he had a great birthday. They had sent Mr. **Rabbar** to pick up his best friends and bring them all the way to Africa to be with him. It was the next best thing to seeing them.

Donod pulled the tarp off the back of the jeep. "Okay, dude. Check it out!"

Otto opened his eyes. There was the biggest birthday cake he had ever seen. It had eight levels, like a gigantic wedding cake. It said "Happy Birthday Otto" of course. On the side of the bottom layer, it said "For Otto Only."

"Whoa, that is a most excellent snack," said *Donod*.

Otto was overwhelmed. Everyone helped lift the other layers off the large bottom section.

"Here's something else the Brit dude sent you," said *Donod*. He gave Otto a strange-looking pair of eyeglasses.

Otto put them on. They had infrared lenses. There was a message written across the bottom layer of cake that only he could see. It read,

Happy Birthday, Jake, our son, who we love more than all the creatures in the four corners of the round globe, even the zebras, even though we really like those a lot. You have saved the world from extinction by fatal fart fumes. We're sure this was a scary day for you, but someday we will all get together and laugh about it, because, let's face it, farts are funny.

Remember when you were little and had a favorite stuffed animal zebra named Polka Dot? We took him when we left home so we could feel close to you, and we didn't know what to get you for your birthday because we didn't know if you liked superhard amazing video games with *1001* levels, so we're giving you back Polka Dot. He's inside this layer of cake.

We are hopeful that this is the last birthday you will celebrate without us. We feel sure that we are closing in on our archenemy, the tall skinny man with the enormous neck and the long dangling head.

Love,
Mom and **Dad**

P.S. Eat these eyeglasses so no one else can read this message.

Otto ate the glasses. They melted in his mouth. He was a little sad, because he

1001, Mom, and Dad are palindromes.

happened to love superhard video games with *1001* levels. Besides, the word *level* was a palindrome and so was *1001*. Oh well.

Otto carefully dug his hands into the middle of the cake layer and scooped out a box. In it was the coolest handheld video game machine he'd ever seen, with a note that said, "Fooled you. Have fun. We're keeping the zebra a little longer."

"*Wow*!" said Otto.

"Way *wow*!" said *Donod*. "Let's party."

Party at Ayamaya's

Even though FooFoo didn't get to make a birthday cake, she did get to eat one. And she managed to come up with about 50 different dishes including honey-buttered meat, meat in milk and ketchup, corn-crusted meat, and the ever popular peanut-butter-glazed meat in milk-and-honey gravy.

The Screaming Oranges provided musical entertainment, with additional guests including *Ayamaya* and a dozen members of his huge family. FiFi tap danced, and the Maasais jumped. They are very talented at jumping, and can sometimes jump up many feet from a standing position.

"*Mellem* jump," said *L'il Mellem*. He jumped around in circles, crashing into

everyone and falling down about 75 times.

"Cool," said **Donod**.

"Way cool," said **Ayamaya**.

Otto wrote a song, and sang lead. The Maasais and FiFi sang backup, **Donod** beat the jeep with his drumsticks, and **Ayamaya** yodeled. That got the lions and hyenas in the bush started. It was a joyous celebration.

Was It a Rat I Saw?
by Otto

(In the note of G)

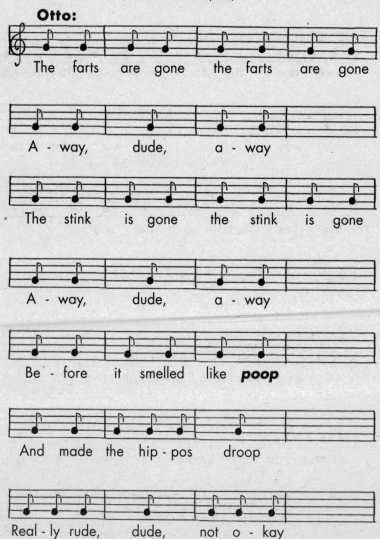

Otto:

The farts are gone the farts are gone

A - way, dude, a - way

The stink is gone the stink is gone

A - way, dude, a - way

Be - fore it smelled like **poop**

And made the hip - pos droop

Real - ly rude, dude, not o - kay

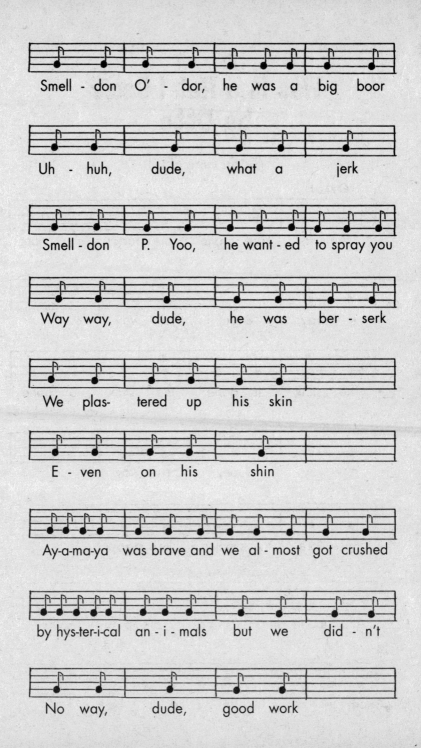

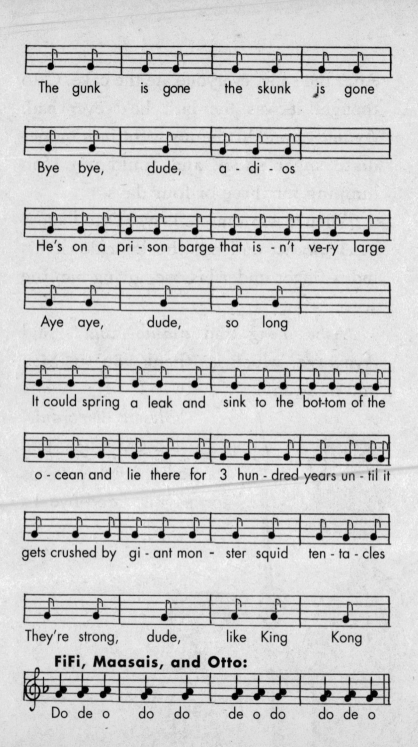

After the song, everyone ate the cake. Otto thought it was the best he'd ever had. *Ayamaya* and his family went into immediate sugar shock and could not stop jumping for three or four days.

When it was time to leave, Otto looked at *Ayamaya* and put the knuckle of his index finger under his *eye*, giving him the secret sign.

"*Ashe oleng* and *asante sana*," said *Ayamaya*, which is "thank you" in Maa and in Swahili.

"*Olesere lemorani*," said Otto, who had learned the Maa words for saying good-bye to someone you greatly respect as a warrior.

Ayamaya gave Otto a huge hug. *"Olesere lemorani,"* he said back, and jumped away into the bush.

Otto Undercover #6:
Brain Freeze

It was Halloween and Otto had three things on his mind. Trick-or-treating, rock and roll, and Raisinets.

Tonight he was trick-or-treating with his best friend, the tiny toddler *L'il Mellem*. Otto and *Mellem* were going to trade in all their lame trick-or-treat loot for the little chocolate-covered raisins and eat them until their stomachs burst.

Otto and Aunt FooFoo had visited 15 stores, and they were all out of Raisinets. Otto was a patient guy, but this was pretty frustrating. He stood in line at the register with a cart full of roasted quail eggs and frozen veal shanks, because his aunt could never go to a store and just get what they came for. A weird guy dressed as a chicken stood behind Otto in line. He had dandruff all over his feathers.

It was Otto's old enemy, the car thief Paulie Prat.